Written by Robert D. Christensen

Illustrated by Rebecca Christensen Wheeler

CFI

Springville, Utah

Text © 2005 Robert D. Christensen
Illustrations © 2005 Rebecca C. Wheeler
All rights reserved.

No part of this book may be reproduced in any form whatsoever, whether by graphic, visual, electronic, film, microfilm, tape recording, or any other means, without prior written permission of the author and illustrator, except in the case of brief passages embodied in critical reviews and articles.

ISBN: 1-55517-864-2
v.1

Published by Cedar Fort,
an imprint of Cedar Fort, Inc.
925 N. Main, Springville, Utah, 84663
www.cedarfort.com

Distributed by:

Jacket design by Nicole Williams
Cover design © 2005 by Lyle Mortimer

Printed in Hong Kong
10 9 8 7 6 5 4 3 2 1

Printed on acid-free paper

To Mom and Dad, who showed their children how to make the world better.

—RDC

To the ones who have made my world such a wonderful place to be: Thomas, Rachel, and Samuel.

—RCW

I think if I were to create a world, it would be exactly like this one. I probably wouldn't make any changes at all because I think this world is terrific just the way it is.

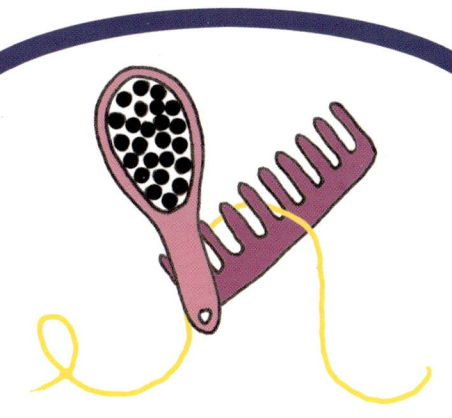

Actually, there's just one minor change I would make. In my world, if you were born with blonde hair it would stay blonde your whole life. It wouldn't turn brown and then white and then fall out. I don't see the point in that.

Also, I wouldn't put hair in people's ears or noses. I don't see the point in that either. So I guess I would make those few minor changes, but otherwise my world would be exactly like this one.

Also, I would make just one other change and add one more hour to each day. People are always saying they wish there were more hours in the day, so I would give them one. And I would make it during the nighttime. Maybe the extra hour of sleep would make the people in my world less grouchy.

Also, I would make one other little change and do birthdays somewhat differently. On their birthday, my people could choose whether they wanted to receive presents and add a year to their lives or give presents and subtract a year from their lives. That would be good. Other than that, my world would be just like this one.

Also, I would totally do away with mosquitoes and hornets. And I would make sure that dinosaurs—at least a few of them—didn't become extinct. That would make zoos way better.

Also, I would design my people with built-in air bags. That would cut way down on emergency room costs. Of course, football wouldn't be as exciting.

Actually, I'll have to think more about that one.

Also, I would make one other change. Since tobacco is really bad for us, I would make tobacco smoke horribly stinky and obnoxious so that my people would know to avoid it. Actually, it already is, so I guess I don't need to make any changes there.

Also, I would put more vitamins and fewer calories in chocolate.

My world would be exactly like this one with those small improvements.

Also, I would pattern my world after the game Monopoly and make sure that every time my people passed "GO," they would get $200. That way everyone would want to keep going even if they were broke.

Also, I would make it so that my animals didn't eat each other. I don't really see why we need a food chain; it causes too much fear. My leopards might chase my deer around, pretending that they were going to eat them, but it would only be for fun because the animals would all just eat grass and leaves.

Also, I would cut down on pain. I know it's useful for helping people avoid harmful things, but I think there's way too much of it. I'm pretty sure my people could get the same message with fewer ouches.

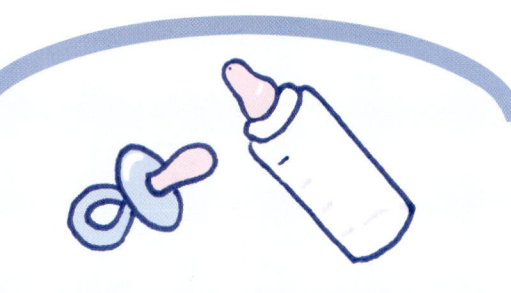

Also, to help the women in my world with labor and delivery, I would make babies weigh only about one pound at birth, but then I would have them grow really fast over the next couple of days.

Day 3

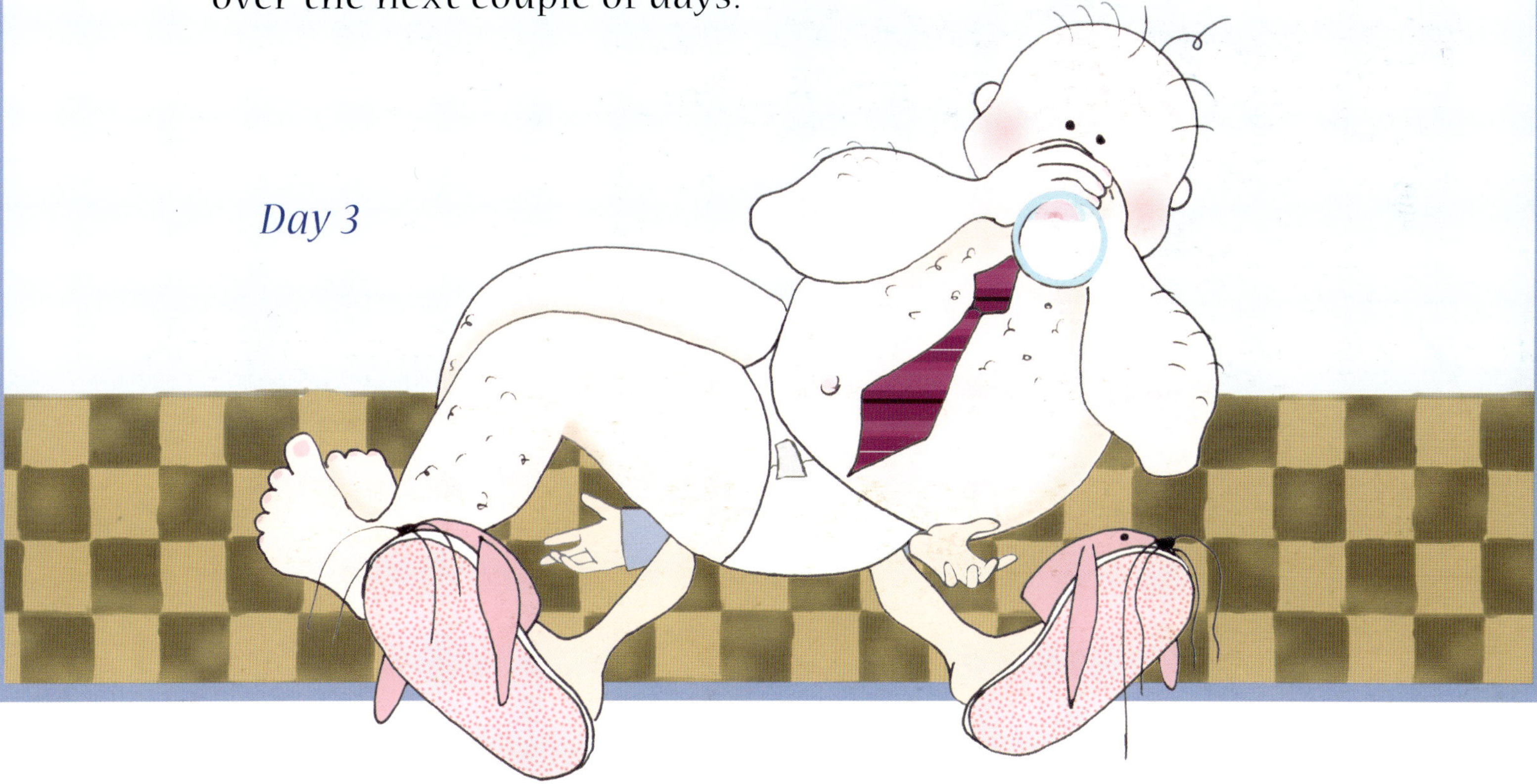

Also, I would give a commandment that you can't eat or chew gum while saying your prayers because the chewing sounds come out louder than your words, and that's rude.

Also, my people would have knees and elbows that bend both ways.

Also, my weeks would all have at least one holiday, two Saturdays, and no Mondays.

Also, all the kids would come in the house when they were called. Otherwise, they'd get an electrical shock.

Actually, after thinking about it, these ideas may not be so great after all. I guess if I were to create a world for me to run, it would be exactly like this one. I probably wouldn't make any changes at all because I think this world is terrific just the way it is.

The End